TWISTAPLOT®
11

AMP-OUT ON DANGER MOUNTAIN

B. B. Hiller

Illustrations by David Tommasino

D1405425

SCHOLASTIC INC.
New York Toronto London Auckland Sydney Tokyo

For my Andy

ISBN 0-590-33102-7

Copyright © 1984 by Barbara B. Hiller. All rights reserved. Published by Scholastic Inc.

12 11 10 9 8 7 6 5 4 3 2 1   8   4 5 6 7 8 9/8

Printed in the U.S.A.   01

BEWARE!!!
DO NOT READ THIS BOOK FROM BEGINNING TO END

You are about to set out on a camping trip like no other you've ever taken before. You'll need more than just a backpack and a sleeping bag. You'd better bring along all the courage you can find, for this camp-out is not a routine class trip. You are headed for mysterious Danger Mountain — where you never know *whom* you might find . . . or *what* might find you!!

If you choose your paths wisely, you can follow the forest trails to fame and fortune. Take a wrong turn, though, and the end of the trail might mean the end of you.

It's up to you. All you have to do is follow the directions at the bottom of each page. But before you make your choices, remember — they don't call it Danger Mountain for nothing!!

Happy trails!

Turn to PAGE 2.

The light of the full moon casts shadows through the forest. Beside you, around the campfire, your friends are dozing or whispering to one another. As you slap another creepy bug crawling on your leg, you wish like crazy that you were back in your own room, playing Zapman.

No such luck. You're on your class trip — a camp-out — and so far, it's a bummer. No excitement at all. You voted to go to AdventureLand, famous for its double loop-the-loop roller coaster, but you lost. The nerds who voted for this camp-out must have been paid off by squadrons of hungry mosquitoes.

You had thought that at least the destination of the camp-out sounded promising — Danger Mountain. But as near as you can figure out, the most dangerous thing about Danger Mountain is the mosquitoes. Shows how much you know.

To your left is Ronnie Newberger with his weird hat pulled down over his ears. He has a strange, contented look on his face. Then you see why. The hat is covering earphones. Ronnie's got a radio and he's turned in to WROC back home. Trust Ronnie to bring civilization to the boondocks!

Turn to PAGE 3.

Maria Dussel stands up to make an announcement about the Tall Tale Contest that is to begin shortly. Maria says her tall tale will be about Chief Sitting Elk who lived on Danger Mountain 200 years ago. The winners of the contest will spend two days at AdventureLand. Now *that's* the best news you've heard all day!

Next, Mr. Marks, the biology teacher and class trip chaperone, announces the schedule for tomorrow. "Six-o'clock, wake-up; six-thirty, bird walk; seven-thirty, breakfast and clean-up; eight-fifteen, 10-mile hike." Blah, blah.

You tune out Mr. Marks' incredibly boring schedule by trying to think up a tall tale to get you to AdventureLand. Unfortunately, your imagination isn't working, except to remind you how good a pizza would taste after those burned franks.

Suddenly, Ronnie's face changes from contented to astonished. "Hey, get this!" he cries, as he pulls off his hat, revealing the earphones. "There are bank robbers round here!"

"Yeah, sure," you say. Ronnie loves to play practical jokes.

"No, really," Ronnie protests. "I'm getting this story on the radio. Listen!"

Want to know more about the bank robbers? Turn to PAGE 4.

"They say that a gang held up the Third National Trust in town this morning," says Ronnie. "They stole $250,000 and were last seen heading west toward the mountain and Lake Pittiwawa. That's here! They are armed and *dangerous*!"

Someone gasps and everyone starts to talk at once.

"Okay, boys and girls," says Mr. Marks in his most irritating, "I'm-in-charge" voice. "I'd better let the authorities know where we are. There's a CB radio in one of the vans and I'm going back out to it. You are all to stay here and wait for me. Under no circumstances are you to leave the campsite." And with that, he takes off alone.

The woods seem a bit darker now and a lot more exciting. After all, you think, there could be bank robbers hiding behind the mosquitoes!

Maria, apparently oblivious to the dangers lurking beyond the campfire, begins telling her tall tale. Nobody pays much attention.

Turn to PAGE 5

Suddenly, everyone is alert. What was that sound? There it is again. It sounds like a person yelling.

"Come on!" says Ronnie. "That could be the bank robbers and it sounds as though they're nearby. I sure don't want to be found by them. Let's get out of here!" Your friend J.J. agrees to go with Ronnie.

"That wasn't a bank robber!" says Leslie Mayhew. "That was Mr. Marks. He must be calling for help. Let's go help him!"

Maria, who resents the interruption of her story, wants all the kids to stay for the Tall Tale Contest.

Now you have to decide:

If you want to run for safety, go with Ronnie and J.J. and turn to PAGE 6.

If you think Mr. Marks may need your help, go with Leslie and turn to PAGE 7.

If you want to stick with Maria and the tall tales, turn to PAGE 20.

"I'm going with Ronnie," you say. You're glad J.J. wants to come along, too. J.J. is very smart and that could be useful. Also, you know from experience that Ronnie can be something of a pain with his practical jokes. So you're relieved to have a good friend along, even if J.J. always insists on lugging around a comic book collection everyplace.

Ronnie and J.J. head out through the woods to the creek. After a moment's hesitation, you follow. The woods are dark and, though you're trying to walk carefully, you keep getting hit by low-hanging branches.

"J.J.!" you say, annoyed. "Stop letting the branches snap in my face!"

"I'm not doing anything to you," J.J. answers from quite a distance. "I'm too far ahead of you. How could I snap branches in your face?"

An excellent question. J.J. is right. There is a big space between you two and Ronnie is in *front* of J.J. So who, or what, is snapping branches in your face, in the dark, in the woods, late at night, far from home????

If you think you'd better find out, turn to PAGE 8.

If you are sure you'll be better off not knowing, turn to PAGE 16.

"Come with us," you say to your good friend, Jackie. "Staying here is crazy."

Jackie agrees and joins you and Leslie. You three decide to follow the trail Mr. Marks took. But no one can remember exactly which trail that was.

Jackie suggests you make a map of the camp area and decide which way to go based on that. It looks like this:

If you think Trail A will get you to Mr. Marks and the vans, turn to PAGE 9.

If you have a hunch that Trail B is the way, turn to PAGE 14.

If Trail C seems right to you, turn to PAGE 17.

Another branch snaps in your face.

"Hey! Who's doing that?" you call.

No answer.

You grope in front of you — unable to see in the pitch-black of the mountain forest. Suddenly, you bump into someone.

"Oooooomph!"

It's not just someone, it's your good old friend J.J., and J.J. is none too pleased. Well, there may have *been* something between you, but whatever it was is gone now.

All of a sudden, a strange cry breaks the stillness. "This way! This way!" calls a nasal voice. It seems to be above you. "This way!" You hear it again. You and J.J. stop to listen.

"Hey! Who's there?" you call, but the only answer you get is "This way!" and now the voice has moved. Who *is* it? J.J. has an idea.

"You know, I think I've got this figured out. All the voice says is 'This way.' It seems to be moving all the time and it's above us. Maybe it's a bird . . . a parrot." Yes, that *would* explain it. But how could there be a parrot so far away from where anyone lives? Parrots that talk usually belong to someone.

Should you follow it?
Yes, turn to PAGE 10.
No, turn to PAGE 12.

Leslie leads the way down the path toward Mr. Marks and the vans — you hope. None of you can really remember how you got into the camp, so it's just a shot in the dark as to how to get home.

"Yeah, a shot in the dark," agrees Jackie. And all of a sudden that's exactly what you hear. *Bang!* You all stop and listen as a voice rings out from a distant bullhorn.

"Attention! We know you are in there. We are searching the mountain with infrared equipment and heat sensitive scopes. Give yourselves up now or we will come after you. We *will* get you — dead or alive!"

What now? You sure don't want the police to mistake you for the bank robbers, but poor Mr. Marks is still out there somewhere and may need your help.

"I think we'd better try to find the police," says Leslie.

"Forget that," says Jackie. "The police are over on the other side of the lake. That's where the voice was coming from. Let's find Mr. Marks and get to the vans!"

If you want to seek the protection of the law, head for the lake on PAGE 70.

If you're still concerned about Mr. Marks, turn to PAGE 72.

"I'm going after that bird," you declare. "Where there's a talking bird, there's an owner." J.J. decides to come, too. Ronnie must have been too far ahead of you to hear the bird. He's probably already at the creek.

You and J.J. walk cautiously toward the bird's call. Now you are pretty sure it is a bird, for you can see a fluttering in the branches.

"This way!" it continues to call. Quietly, you and J.J. sneak up on it. You both stand behind a tree to wait for the next call, but it's not the bird you hear. This time it's a woman's voice. "This way!"

Then you hear the bird again, crying loudly, "No! No! Go away! Run for your lives!"

"What does a bird know," says J.J. "Let's see who's calling now."

If you want to run for your life, turn to PAGE 30.

If you want to go toward the woman's voice, turn to PAGE 41.

As you float along downstream, you realize that it doesn't matter which turn you take, you are hopelessly lost inside Danger Mountain! How well it was named! It's a good thing you like to swim because it looks as if you're going to be doing it until

THE END

"Let's get out of here!" says Ronnie and he begins running toward the creek. You and J.J. run after him. Bird or no bird, you're scared. Who wouldn't be???

When you are safely away from the "bird," you and your friends climb on to a rock to get a view of the creek. There it is, the moonlight sparkling on the water. It's quite beautiful and you'd probably enjoy it if you didn't have the creepy feeling a gang of bank robbers is about to appear.

You can hear splashing — more than just the water bubbling over the rocks. Is it the robbers, or the police, or your classmates wandering in the woods? You grip the rock tightly. You don't want to admit you're frightened, but your knuckles are definitely white.

Suddenly, the rock shifts. All three of you hold tight. The rock cracks open to reveal a deep cave in the mountain. A strong light flickers below.

Now you can hear voices to accompany the splashing in the creek.

Should you go into the cave and hide from whoever is walking in the creek? Turn to PAGE 84.

Should you stay by the creek and hide from whoever is in the cave? Turn to PAGE 47.

Okay, so you, Leslie, and Jackie decide to follow this trail into the woods.

There's always something exciting about walking in the woods, day or night. It makes you feel as if you are the first person ever in an uncharted land. You have visions of Pocahontas and Captain Smith — maybe even Christopher Columbus. What adventure!

Suddenly an unpleasant odor reaches your nose. An odor no doubt familiar even to Christopher C., but one that probably means you've gone the wrong way. You've come to the latrine. Phew!

You'd better go back to PAGE 7 and try another trail.

Okay, you're going to go for a torch.

First, you catch J.J.'s eye and then look
at the torches. Then you muster every
ounce of courage you have and scream as
loudly as you can. While your captors close
in to quiet you, J.J. goes for a torch — only
to be stopped by a fourth man who steps
out of the shadows. You hadn't seen him
before.

"Quiet!" he yells. So much for that bright
idea.

"Are you the bank robbers?" asks Ronnie.

"Bank robbers? Hardly! We're anthropologists from State University. We're on
a field trip, seeking the truth behind the
legend of the ghost of Chief Sitting Elk."

"Uh, sure," you say, not sure at all. "If
you are anthropologists, not bank robbers,
and we're kids, not Chief Sitting Elk, why
are you pointing those weapons at us? Why
are you holding us captive?"

"Because we thought you were — "

Suddenly, there is a strong gust of stale,
dry air. It blows out all of the torches and
dims the fire in the cave. Where did it come
from? Could it be the ghost of Sitting Elk?

If you think it's Sitting Elk, turn to PAGE
5.

If you think there must be some other
explanation, turn to PAGE 57.

16

Ignore the branches snapping in you face? Are you crazy? Do you know wh kind of stuff you could find on a mounta at night? Bears, wolves, and wildcats, ju for starters. There are bank robbers o there, too, remember?

You'd better give up now, because wi that attitude, it will surely soon be

THE END

P.S. Or you could rethink this and go o to PAGE 8.

Yes, this seems to be the right trail back to the vans. Jackie was smart to make the map.

You're feeling pretty smug as you walk through the forest, certain you're headed for the vans, home, and safety, and away from Danger Mountain.

Suddenly without warning you see Leslie's hand go up as a signal to stop. Jackie stops next, as Leslie groans, "Oh, *no!*"

You and Jackie see, too. It's Mr. Marks. He is lying across the trail in what appears to be a *most* uncomfortable position, eyes fixed toward the sky.

While you are gathered around him, wondering what to do or say, Mr. Marks' eyes suddenly focus on you. His hand goes to his mouth in the classic teacher gesture.

"Shhhhhhhhhhhhh!" he hisses at you. "Don't say anything!"

If you think he's saying that because he's a teacher and that's what teachers always say, turn to PAGE 19.

If you think he knows what he's hissing about, turn to PAGE 25.

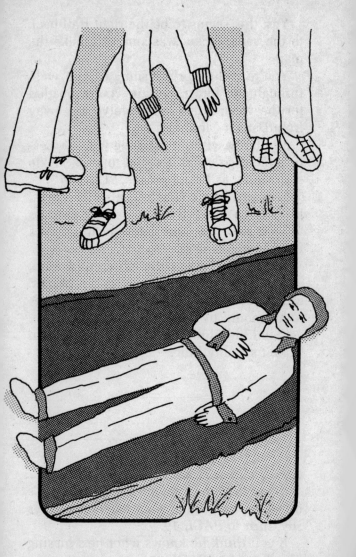

"Mr. Marks," you say. "This is not a classroom and you don't have to tell us to be quiet. We're out in the middle of the woods. You obviously tripped on something and got knocked out. Clearly, you've become slightly unglued. Don't worry, though. Jackie, Leslie, and I will take care of you. I took a first-aid course so I know just what to do. . . ." You notice that you have lost your audience. Everyone is looking at a point behind you.

"Shut up, kid," orders a menacing voice. You turn around, a sinking feeling in the pit of your stomach. You don't have to look twice. It's the bank robbers, all right.

"Oh, boy!" you say, thinking fast. "Are we glad to see you!" Everyone looks a bit surprised, but you've got a plan up your sleeve. You look the leader right in the eye.

"There's something I've got to tell you. It's . . ."

___

You've got a chance, a slim one, to scare them off.

If you think you can convince them the police are coming, turn to PAGE 21.

If you think you can make them believe they've been exposed to bubonic plague, turn to PAGE 23.

Hang around the campfire when there are bank robbers in the woods? Come now, where is your sense of adventure?

Go back to PAGE 5 and choose something else.

You've got their attention. The question is: Can you con a con man? Here goes nothing.

"Okay, kid," says one of the bank robbers. "What have you got to tell us?"

"Well, we've been playing the game and doing it pretty well, but now our leader hurt himself and I was afraid we would miss our rendezvous with Dad's platoon, so I'm glad to find you." You're talking very tough. "Which platoon are you with?"

"Huh?" You've got him hooked. Now, to pull in the line.

"You know, for the Danger Mountain Navigation Night — the annual contest between you police officers and the local Scout troops. I guess Dad's platoon must have sent you guys to this meeting point. Are we late? I thought we would be here about five minutes before Dad's platoon, but it looks like you beat us."

The robbers look at one another. You can almost see the wheels turning in their brains.

"Well, no," answers the leader slowly. "This isn't actually our rendezvous. We got a little sidetracked. We're really supposed to be about a quarter of a mile from here and we'd better get going so we're not late."

Turn to PAGE 22.

"Do me a favor," he adds, completely convinced he's got you fooled now. "When your dad's platoon shows up, don't tell them we were here. I don't want those guys to know we goofed."

"You can count on it!" you tell him, but he hardly hears you, he is so busy chasing after his buddies.

You three help Mr. Marks to his feet now.

"Come on, let's get to the vans quickly so we can really contact the police," you say. Off you go, and 200 yards along the trail, you find the vans. One has a CB radio that Leslie knows how to use. Pretty soon, the place *is* swarming with police platoons, waiting for a rendezvous with the bank robbers.

The picture of you and your friends that appears in the newspaper a few days later may not do you justice, but the story under it calls you a local hero. That's a lot nicer than a "fast-talking liar," which is what the bank robber calls you at the police station.

Congratulations, local hero!

THE END

Okay, you've seen enough of *General Hospital* to make this look real. Here goes.

"What I want to tell you is that we need your help!" Your friends and Mr. Marks look at you as if you're crazy.

"Our teacher is sick! Look at him! We have to get him back to town. I don't know how much you know about the plague, but when it hits, it hits fast. If we don't get him to the hospital fast, we're all done for! If you'll help us, we've got a chance. A small one, but a ch —"

The robber cuts you off.

"Shut up, kid! Your teacher was KO'ed because I hit him, not because of some cockamamie disease he don't have."

Mr. Marks pulls himself up, rubbing the back of his head. He pats you on the shoulder and thanks you for trying.

You are waiting to hear what the bank robbers have in mind when, suddenly, lights start flashing above you. First to the left, then to the right. There's a loud, high-pitched whine that's growing louder by the minute.

"Hey, guys," says the robber. "That's a police chopper!"

Go to PAGE 24.

"I don't know how the cops found us, but they did. Let's scram. Take the loudmouth as a hostage!" Alas, he's pointing to you. One of the other robbers grabs you.

"Ah-choo! Ah-choo!" you start sneezing uncontrollably. "I must be allergic to your aftershave lotion," you tell your captor. "Ah-choo! Ah-choo!"

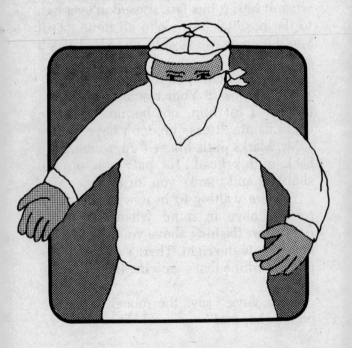

If you have any allergies, turn to PAGE 27.

If you don't, turn to PAGE 92.

Mr. Marks hisses "Shhhhh!" again with such authority that you and your friends freeze. His eyes search the branches and sky above him. You look up also, expecting to see the bank robbers. But wait a minute. Who ever heard of bank robbers in trees?

Mr. Marks stands up, shaking his head.

"Oh, I'm so disappointed," he says. "I thought for a moment — just a moment! — that I heard the mating call of the rare Thompson's red-billed night duck! Can you imagine? It nests in tall pines, and although I know it would be most unusual in this zone, I hoped against hope that I had actually — "

"Mr. Marks, have you lost your marbles?" Leslie asks bluntly. "These woods are full of bank robbers and you're looking for red-nosed ducks? Let's get on to the vans! Here, this is the way to go." Leslie points to the left.

"Oh, no," says Mr. Marks. "Where we want to go is to the right!"

If you want to stick with Leslie, go left, to PAGE 14.

If you think Mr. Marks really isn't a bird brain, go right, to PAGE 31.

"Don't move!" you whisper to your friends. They nod in agreement.

"Look over there," says one of the robbers. Uh-oh! This is it. They've seen you and you're in trouble. The robbers step out of the creek to take a look at you. They are surprised to have three kids on their hands, but soon they are surprised by something else.

"Freeze," says a third voice. "This is the police. Drop your weapons."

You've probably been thinking they only say that in movies, but here they are, for real, saving your skin and capturing the bank robbers!

All right!

THE END

"Ah-choo!" you say, again.

"God bless you," says Leslie.

"Gesundheit," says Jackie.

"Shut up, kid," says the bank robber.

"Ah-choo!"

"I said shut up!" warns the robber.

"Hey, that wasn't me that time!" you say.

"Ah-choo!" There it is again.

"Huh?" says the bank robber. Everyone looks up. That last sneeze sounded like it came from the helicopter.

The lights above you grow brighter and the whine from the machine becomes even louder. You all squint at the lights, trying to see the helicopter. Suddenly, you realize that it is definitely not a helicopter. It's not a plane, nor a bird, nor anything else you've ever seen on this earth!

"It's a UFO," you cry.

"Ah-choo!" says the UFO, as if to agree.

So, now you've got bank robbers who don't trust you on your left; a teacher and friends who think you've gone bats on your right; and a — get this — a UFO with the flu above you. Swell.

This is going to call for some very delicate maneuvering.

If you want to scream for help as loudly as you can, turn to PAGE 87.

If you figure the only way out is a dead faint, turn to PAGE 77.

"Last one in is a rotten egg!" you cry and run for the underground creek.

Ronnie and J.J. look a bit confused, but then they decide to trust you. First, J.J. checks the zipper on the waterproof knapsack that holds the comic book collection (J.J. has a weird side), then they both jump into the water after you. The strange men start to follow, but the strong current of the creek sweeps you out of the large room of the cave before they can do anything. Soon, you come to a still pool where two branches of the creek converge.

"Look," you say while treading water. "This water got in here somehow. It's got to get out of here, right?"

J.J.'s faith in you is fading fast. "You mean I've put my whole comic book collection in jeopardy on a hunch? Haven't you ever heard of underground streams? They can run under a mountain like this for miles and *miles*!"

"Well," you answer J.J. "There may be underground streams, but are there any underground McDonalds?" Ronnie and J.J. stare at you until you point to a Big Mac container floating toward you.

"Freedom's this way!" you say, and you begin swimming upstream.

Go to PAGE 29.

You really think that the creek *will* go above the ground and that you'll go with it. But the fact is that a Big Mac container can do a lot of things a kid can't. Like go through a teeny space or stay under water for a *very* long time. What have you gotten everyone into? You keep your fears to yourself, though. You don't want your friends to be as scared as you are.

Suddenly, the air is not so cool, the water not so smooth. You come to the opening of the cave and you hear voices! At first, you want to call for help, but so far tonight, this forest hasn't been exactly full of neighborly types. Caution seems advisable. You wait for Ronnie and J.J. at the mouth of the cave.

"There are people up there," you announce. "Let's climb onto this rock and see if they are friend or foe before we identify ourselves."

You stand as quietly as you can, listening to the voices. It's the men from the cave, and one is showing the others where the creek comes above ground. They have followed you!

Where to, now?

Want to go back into the cave? Turn to PAGE 82.

Want to try to sneak away from the men in the woods? Turn to PAGE 32.

"J.J.! Let's get out of here!" J.J. decides you're right and you both turn and run away from those creepy voices as fast as you can. You don't have to go very far before you come to a large rock. The two of you duck behind it panting nervously.

Soon you hear a rustling in the leaves and a funny — almost human — sound.

You both freeze. The sound is familiar — almost like a laugh — a very weird one. All of a sudden, Ronnie is beside you, clutching his sides and laughing hysterically.

"Gee, Ronnie, what's the big idea sneaking up on us, and what's so funny?" you ask.

Ronnie squinches up his face and says in a now too familiar voice: "*This* way!" Good old Ronnie the practical joker. So funny you forgot to laugh.

"Let's get to the creek," says J.J. "It's this way."

"No, it's not. It's this way," Ronnie counters.

Whom do you trust?

If you believe J.J., go to PAGE 75.

If you're foolish enough to think Ronnie knows what he's doing, turn to PAGE 63.

If you want to give up on those jokers and find your way back to the campsite, turn to PAGE 40.

"Okay, kids, just follow me over here, to the right a bit," says Mr. Marks, and off you go. He seems to know what he is doing. Unfortunately, though, there is no sign of the vans and the woods are getting thicker and darker.

Mr. Marks holds up his hand for you to stop. You and Jackie stand still.

"There it is! Look at that!" Mr. Marks whispers.

"What?"

"Just over the rise in that pine tree is the duck I was talking about — Thompson's red-billed. . ." He creeps up the rise then lunges ahead. Suddenly, you can't see him at all. That may be a blessing. Nevertheless. . .

Then, you hear his loud cry, "Aaaaaaaarghhhh!" You and Jackie run up the rise to help, but you find you're not going to be much use, because there you are, in mid-air, too! You've fallen off the same cliff Mr. Marks went over. You can see the bottom rushing toward you. Is there any hope???

There is hope if you can say "Thompson's red-billed night duck" three times before you hit the bottom of the cliff. Turn to PAGE 35 to see if you made it.

Just as you think you might have a chance to escape those weirdos, you hear the words you were dreading.

"Here they are!" You are really trapped this time for, instead of bows and arrows, the men have guns. One of them is also carrying a backpack.

"All right, kids," says one of the men. "We don't want to harm you. We just want to incapacitate you temporarily. Do as you're told and you'll be fine."

"Are you the bank robbers? Is that the money?" you ask.

"Kid, don't ask questions. The less you know, the better off you'll be." So that answers *those* questions. Now for the next one.

"How come you had bows and arrows in the cave?"

"Bows and arrows? Oh, those were just tent poles! Really scared you with them, didn't we? Look," he continued. "All we want is to keep you from getting us caught. What we're going to do is to tie you to this tree. Your friends will find you in the morning, but by then we'll be safely in the next state."

Turn to PAGE 33

Well, things could be worse, but you sure are going to be uncomfortable. Something occurs to you.

"At least let J.J. take off the backpack," you say.

"Sure, sure, kid."

"I'll help," you volunteer. And you do. Shortly thereafter you find yourselves tied and waiting through a long night. There's a small consolation, though.

By the time the sun is rising, Mr. Marks and a squad of police find the three of you, sleeping fitfully, tied to the tree. What a relief to be released. You explain what happened and the police radio the information to their relay squad.

"Thanks, kids," says one of the police. "The robbers got away with the money, but since you heard them say they were headed to the next state, we know where to look."

"You're very welcome," you say coolly. "But you're not entirely correct. They may have gotten away, but they didn't get away with the money.

That's a pretty clever thing to say, but what are you talking about? Turn to PAGE 34 to find out!

Everyone looks at you.

"It's over there. J.J. has it in that back-pack." The police take the pack and open it to find $250,000!

"You see," you explain, "I noticed that the robbers had their loot in a pack identical to the one J.J. uses to hold the comics. I helped J.J. remove the pack and then I made a switch!" Everyone is amazed at how devilishly clever you are — everyone except J.J. who is extremely annoyed at having lost all those comics.

"Never mind," you console J.J. "You'll be able to replace the collection twice over with the reward money!"

When you're right, you're right!

THE END

Did you think it was rather strange when Mr. Marks said his red-billed night duck was perched in a tree? That's ridiculous, of course. Ducks don't nest in pine trees. They have webbed feet and can't possibly stand on the branches.

Note that in the above paragraph, you've been doing a lot of thinking. That's because you've got a lot of time. You stopped your fall off Danger Mountain by grabbing onto the branches of a little tree. You're now standing on a very narrow ledge.

Jackie, who also got a hold of the little tree, is peering over the edge of the ledge.

"You know," says Jackie, "Mr. Marks is on a ledge about 20 feet below us and he's okay, but I've been thinking. There's something fishy about him."

Two great minds with a single thought. Actually, two thoughts: 1) Mr. Marks is hiding something; and 2) How are you going to get off the ledge to safety?

Which problem would you like to start with?

Mr. Marks? Turn to PAGE 91.

The cliff? Turn to PAGE 36.

"Look!" says Jackie. "I think I see a way out of here."

"Sky hooks?"

"No, I mean it. Perhaps a mountain climber was practicing scaling the mountain, because there are metal spikes — pitons — sticking out, and they lead to the top. It's almost like a ladder. Let's go!" Why not, you think. You call to Mr. Marks and point out the pitons. He yells that he'll meet you at the top.

As you climb up, you make the terrible mistake of looking down to see how the others are doing. They are fine, but the rocky chasm, so deep below you, makes your stomach queasy and the world starts spinning.

"Look up!" Jackie reminds you — just in time. The mountain climbing life is *not* for you. At last, you are safe. Soon, Jackie and Mr. Marks arrive, too. You catch your breath, and then face the inevitable.

"Mr. Marks, about that so-called Thompson's red-billed night duck?"

Mr. Marks looks a bit resigned, "Well, kids," he begins. "You're probably not going to believe this, but . . ."

Do you think you're going to believe him this time?

Yes? Turn to PAGE 86.

No? Turn to PAGE 89.

"Let's get out of here," you whisper to your friends. They nod in agreement and you begin moving away from the creek, carefully, quietly. Then you hear one of the men's voices.

"Here it is, on the left." That was your rock he was pointing at. You're relieved that there's a good 10 feet between you and the rock now! Stealthily the three of you creep away. You know that the *worst* thing you could do now is to make noise.

Crash! Clang! You trip, twisting your ankle, and a huge supply of change falls out of your pocket.

"What was that?" calls a robber.

"I don't know, but we'd better find out!"

The men start toward you.

If they find you, you'll be done for! You'll be a hostage — or worse! Is there any way out? You start gathering up your change.

Quick! Figure out the sum of three quarters, one dime, one nickel, and three pennies and turn to that page to see what happens.

You and Jackie swing out and back several times, going higher each time, but still getting nowhere near the top.

"Uh, swell idea, Jackie," you say. "I mean it's lots of fun — much better than the playground, but still . . ."

"I don't know how to make it swing higher," Jackie moans.

"Maybe we don't *have* to make it swing higher," you realize suddenly. "Why don't we skip the Tarzan stuff and just climb up it?"

You should have thought of that in the first place. Not only can you get up, but the vine also reaches to Mr. Marks' ledge and pretty soon you're all at the top.

Now it's Mr. Marks' turn. You and Jackie look at him expectantly, as he says, "Well, kids, you're probably not going to believe this, but . . ."

If you think it's about time somebody told the truth, turn to PAGE 86.

If you think this'll be another whopper, turn to PAGE 89.

Lightning.

Did you think of lightning? No? Well, see? The saying is right. There you are, suspended in mid-air when, suddenly, the sky is completely illuminated with sixteen zillion volts of electricity, headed straight for you. What a shocking ending!

THE END

40

"Forget it, you two," you tell Ronnie and J.J. "This is crazy! You two can wander around the woods all you want. I'm going back to the campsite. At least I'll know where I am, and there's a better chance I'll get out of these woods alive!" You turn around and try to retrace your steps.

Fortunately, it works. Soon you can hear the kids still around the campfire. As you walk in, Leslie Mayhew calls out —

"Oh, I'm so glad you're here! Mr. Marks still hasn't come back and we don't know where he is or what might have happened to him. I don't want to go after him alone. Will you come with me?"

Well, wandering around the woods with one bunch of nuts got you nowhere. What's wrong with trying it with *another* bunch of nuts?

Turn to PAGE 7.

"Well," you say to J.J. "I wish we *could* see who is calling, but it's still so *dark* in these woods. I don't think it's Ronnie."

"The sun will be up soon."

"Only if I decide to let it come up!" says a woman's voice.

You and J.J. stop dead in your tracks. You can feel the hairs on the back of your neck begin to rise.

"Where are you? *Who* are you?" you ask.

"I'm right beside you," she says, sweetly. And she is. You turn your head to see a woman so pale she almost seems transparent. In fact she looks a lot like the lady on the White Rock bottles — only no wings.

"It's harder to tell you *who* I am, though," she continues. "Some call me a witch. Some call me a hermit. Some say I'm a mad woman. Call me what you wish, but understand this: I rule the forest and *all* that is within."

"Does that include us?" J.J. asks.

"But of course." The woman closes her eyes, as if to concentrate. You begin to get a funny, light-headed feeling. Then light-shouldered, then light-bodied. The gist of it is that soon you are floating in mid-air and J.J. is right next to you. As the sun comes up over the edge of Danger Mountain, so do you!

Turn to PAGE 42.

"J.J.! What's going on?" you cry.

"Psychokinesis. She just thought us into the air. But forget *that*. Look over there!"

You really have a bird's-eye view. To one side, you can see the police searching through the forest. On the other side of you is another group — the bank robbers! Right between the two — in their paths — is the campsite. You've got friends there and they could get hurt. You need help — fast!

If you think you can get the witch to help, turn to PAGE 44.

If you're going to have to outsmart her, turn to PAGE 66.

"Come up here, and take a look at this!" you call to the woman.

"I can see it from here," she tells you. You can believe that! "I suppose I will have to help the police and your friends. But I can only move so much at once. Would you be good enough to hold onto this tree top while I cope with the rest of this mess?"

With that, you are shifted to the branch of a tall white oak. Gravity returns to normal and you hold on tight while you watch the goings-on below with fascination.

As your witch friend goes into a trance, one of the robbers suddenly turns and punches the one next to him. Number three goes after number four. The fifth one jumps on the leader. Soon they are all tumbling on the ground, too busy to notice their money-filled sacks floating in the air toward the campsite and your friends.

"There," says the woman. "That should solve everything. The bank robbers will destroy one another and your friends will be rich!"

"Yeah," you say. "Until the police find our friends with the cash and decide *they* robbed the bank!"

"You don't *like* what I did?" she asks threateningly.

Want to apologize? Turn to PAGE 46.
If not, turn to PAGE 88.

"Aaahooooooooo!" The howling silences everyone. Then after a moment the torches relight by themselves.

"This must be it!" says one of the men. "That's the ghost they've been telling us about. It's Chief Sitting Elk!"

None of this makes much sense to you.

"What on *earth* is going on here?" you ask politely.

"Well," one of the scientists explains, "there is this legend. It seems that Chief Sitting Elk once ruled all the Indian nations in these parts. He was greatly revered, very powerful — and very wealthy. When the settlers came and said they wanted to make peace with the Indians, many of Sitting Elk's people wanted to sign the treaties. Sitting Elk, however, felt this would be dangerous. He wanted his people to continue living as they always had — secluded from outside influences. There was a rebellion among the tribes and when it became clear Sitting Elk would lose, he took all his wealth, and his few remaining followers, and moved into these mountain caves. The story is that the Indians all died out, but the ghost of Sitting Elk remains to protect his treasure from outsiders."

Do you believe this?
If you do, turn to PAGE 49.
If not, turn to PAGE 52.

"Oh, no, I'm sorry," you gulp. I didn't mean to criticize you in *any* way. I think what you did was *wonderful.* Our friends will love it and the bank robbers really *are* done for. It was just fantastic and I hope you didn't misunderstand my little comment — just a joke. You really are very talented." Okay, okay, stop already. Don't lay it on too thick. This lady is *not* dumb.

"Thank you," she says, calmed. "You see, you underestimated me. Your friends now truly *believe* that *they* found the bank robbers. I have altered their memories. They will tell the police how they stopped the robbers and recovered the stolen money. Your friends will get the reward the bank has offered and become rich and famous. Would you like to join them?"

If you'd like to be in on that reward, turn to PAGE 48.

If you think staying with this lady a bit longer has its own rewards, turn to PAGE 50.

You, Ronnie, and J.J. flatten yourselves
against the rock and listen, petrified. More
splashes. Then voices. At first, they are in-
distinguishable, but soon you can hear the
conversation.

"So, where's this place?"

"Up here, somewhere. There's a big rock.
It hides the entrance to a cave. We can go
in there and make the split."

Sounds like the bank robbers are going
to stop for a while. That should give you a
chance to slip away — maybe into the — uh
oh! You realize that you are leaning on the
rock they are looking for. Ronnie and J.J.
realize it, too.

*Do you want to run for it? Turn to PAGE
37.*

*Do you think there may be another big
rock covering a cave entrance? Turn to
PAGE 26.*

"Reward? Sure we'd like to be in on that." You turn to your friend. "Right, J.J.?"

"Right."

"Okay, just relax now and here you go," the woman tells you.

The world seems to spin a bit and you get a nice dizzy feeling. The next thing you know, you're sitting next to J.J. by the campfire and there are the police walking down the path toward you. You and your friends jump up and run to them. There's something you want to tell them, but you're not sure what it is. Then you remember.

"Gee, officer," you say. "What a night! You'll find the robbers over the hill. Here's the money we took from them. What a fight!" Suddenly, the whole struggle with the robbers is very vivid in your memory. In fact, it's the only part of the whole night you remember. You look at J.J., but J.J.'s too busy recounting all those exact same details about the bank robbers to the police. Was there something else you wanted to remember? Hmmmm. . . . It can't have been very important.

Well, the police got the robbers and you got your part of the reward. That sure sounds like a happy ending. Funny, though, how you can't help but think there was something else special about that night!

THE END

You actually believe that? Sounds as if you'll believe *anything*. Here's some advice. While there may be some truth in a legend like that, rarely is the whole thing true. So, now, armed with that bit of wisdom, develop a healthy sense of skepticism and turn to PAGE 52.

"No thanks," you tell the woman. "It's not fair to horn in on their reward."

"How thoughtful of you," she says. "Why don't you come down now. I'd like to show you around my little home."

She takes you both into a cave you hadn't even noticed before and begins showing you her tools.

"Here, this is the mainframe," she says. "I tried to make do with a mini, but I need too much memory. Here's the disk drive and the two back-ups. Just in case, you know. Here's the lab to make chips. This is the microprocessor I use on the trail, but I've been having trouble with the hook-up."

"You've got to be kidding, lady!" says J.J. "This is all state-of-the-art stuff. Twenty-first century technology. Where did this stuff come from?"

"What were you expecting to find here? Eye of newt and toe of frog? That stuff went out with black robes and pointy hats! I built my computer with the help of a couple of how-to books and a mail order catalog."

Something catches your eye. "What's behind this red door?" you ask, politely.

"No! No! Don't go in there!" she cries.

Is she hiding something? Turn to PAGE 56.

Is she really afraid for your safety? Turn to PAGE 59.

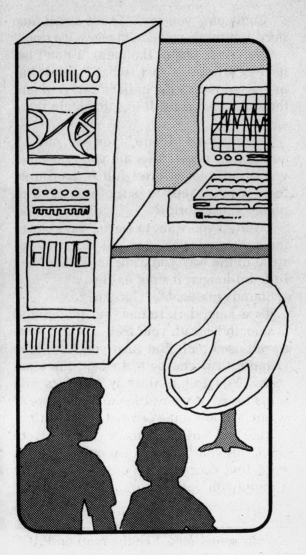

"Come on," you say. "That's a real nice story, but surely you don't believe it's true!"

"No," says one of the men. "I don't believe it's true. In fact, what I think has happened is that the Indians survived and their descendants still live, today, in these caves."

"Let's get out of here," you say, and J.J. and Ronnie agree. After all, you remember you've still got a forest full of bank robbers. Who wants to stick around with phony ghost stories?

"Well, if you want to leave," says one of the anthropologists, "go out that way instead of the way you came in. While it's a little bit longer, it's not as steep."

Sounds reasonable. Out you go.

It's a long, dark tunnel, but the ground is smooth beneath your feet — as if it were a well-used path. But then you find there is more than one path. In fact, there are many. You follow the cave's twists and turns for what seems like hours, unsure of where you are going or what you will find.

You and your friends are getting very tired, but you have to keep on going. You must find your way out of the cave. Trace a route with your finger.

Your route looks like the map on PAGE 53.

The map above shows where you are. If you come out at Exit A, turn to PAGE 65.

If you come out at Exit B, turn to PAGE 54.

If you come out at Exit C, turn to PAGE 81.

After the long trek through the cave without any lights and without any idea where you will end up, it's good to feel the fresh air as you approach the cave's opening.

"Hey, look ahead!" you call. "We're at the end! We've made it!" There's a strange silence. You look behind you to be sure your friends are there, but they are not.

"Hey!" you call.

No answer.

"Where are you?" you yell.

No answer.

"Help!!!" you scream.

No answer.

Where on earth could your friends be? What could have happened to th —

Quick! Turn to PAGE 55.

You freeze in your tracks. As you look down at your feet, your heart lurches into your throat. There, staring straight at you and hissing menacingly, is the poisonous cave viper! There's no place to run and even if there were, you couldn't run fast enough to beat the speed and deadly aim of the cave viper. He got your friends and now he's going to get you! Sorry, this is

THE END

56

Your keen observation skills have grasped the fact that although there's a lot of machinery in the cave, there is no hum of efficient operation and no flashing lights. Everybody knows big machines have flashing lights. There's something phony going on here!

"J.J.! Come here!" you call. Together you burst through the red door. Ah! That's more like it! There are shelves filled with jars of disgusting slimy-looking things. Several tables are covered with beakers of bubbling solutions connected by glass tubes. Two cabinets are stuffed full of bottles holding sparkling powders and murky liquids. In one corner stands a bookshelf, edged with lacy cobwebs and packed with ancient, musty, leather-bound volumes. A *real* sorcerer's laboratory!

The woman follows you into the lab. You turn to her and say, "You, madam, are a phony!"

Now, was that a smart thing to say? Turn to PAGE 60 and find out!

Who cares where that gust of air came from? These guys are as phony as a three dollar bill and you'd better get away from them — *if you can!*

While the men look around the cave for the source of the air, you, Ronnie, and J.J. decide to make your escape. You climb back up the path as quickly as you can. Fortunately, the rock is still open at the entrance. When you are all out you push the rock back into place, closing off the cave. The men call out after you, something about beware of something or other, but you can't hear them. It can't possibly matter, can it?

It *certainly* can't matter as much as what's happening now, for in front of you appears . . . a ghost!! A mist surrounds a large, white, formless being. You hear an ominous bellow:

"BEWARE THE ANGER OF CHIEF SITTING ELK!"

What's going on here? Turn to PAGE 58 to find out!

58

"J.J.!" you cry. "Did you see that ghost? Where did it come from?"

"That's what I'm looking into," J.J. assures you and Ronnie. "Look what I've found — a tape recorder, origin of the ghostly voice; a projector, origin of the image; and a fan, origin of the rush of air. I think someone is fooling those guys in there and they've taken the bait. The woods are full of weirdos tonight! I bet *we* could fool those guys in there, too. Want to have some fun?"

Is this your idea of fun?

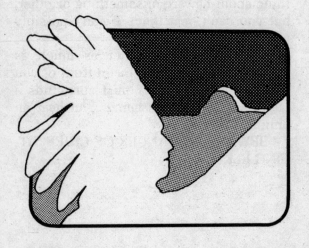

If you want to stay around with the old Indian legend, turn to PAGE 74.

If you want to get back to your friends and Mr. Marks and the bank robbers, turn to PAGE 63.

"Come on, J.J. Let's find out what's in here!"

You push open the door, ignoring the woman's screams.

Well, curiosity killed the cat and it looks like it's going to get you, too! You forgot that to run all that electronic gear requires a lot of electricity. Now, you've found the source and it's giving you the shock of your life!

THE END

"Oh, I *so* hoped you wouldn't find this lab," she says, now nearly in tears. "I've tried so hard to modernize my techniques. I'd love to chuck all these old jars into the garbage, but I've got to make a living! I'm tired of trapping newts just to get their eyes. Do you know how slimy they are? And, I've gotten hundreds of warts from those awful toads. This sorcery business is boring. If only I could get my computer to work!"

"J.J. here is pretty good with computers. Maybe we can help you — it's worth a try, right?" She nods and tries to get the computer to work. Nothing happens.

"Where's the ON switch?" asks J.J.

"The what?" Ah, well, there's her problem, then. She just never turned the computer on! A brief search reveals switches to the left of the main keyboard and on the rear of the CPU. Soon, she's in business.

"I don't know how to thank you," she says.

"It was nothing," you tell her. "But we could use a lift home, please." She nods and closes her eyes. You and J.J. get that light feeling. Within seconds, you are in the center of town, within easy walking distance from home.

"Weird," says J.J. You agree, but you still don't know *how* weird!

Turn to PAGE 61.

Well, that was quite a camp-out, but it's over. Soon, your adventure is just a pleasant memory, until one day you get a letter:

CONGRATULATIONS! You are the winner of a $5,000 prize in the Columbia Publications Sweepstakes! To claim your prize, call this number: 555-1467.

You call the number and find that it's true! The check is being sent to you now! Boy, you just have to call J.J. about this!

"You'll never guess what I just got! I won $5,000!"

"Me, too!"

"Really???" What a coincidence. Or *is* it a coincidence? You know, all these sweepstakes things are done by computer. The computer picks the winners out of all the entries. But you and J.J. didn't enter, so how could you win? Well, a friendly computer could do it, couldn't it? It's a sure bet that a newt's eye couldn't!

THE END

Ah, what a relief to be out of the creepy woods, away from the robbers, police, and who knows what else.

Pretty soon, Mr. Marks returns from the vans.

"Well, I got to a radio," he tells you. "Ronnie was right about the bank robbers, but it seems that the police have now caught them. You know, they didn't even have a real gun with them. It was a cap pistol and some firecrackers! Anyway, the woods are safe now. Let's hit the hay so we can be fresh in the morning for the bird walk. Boy, I *love* a good bird walk, don't you?"

Maybe. Adventure has its place, but there *is* something comfortable about nice, square old Mr. Marks. "Hit the hay...." sounds good.

THE END

"I think we ought to find Mr. Marks and get the police, don't you?" you ask.

You both look at Ronnie, but weird old Ronnie, it appears, is at it again. At first, he's just giggling, but soon he is so convulsed with laughter that he can't stand up. Tears roll down his cheeks. You are about to ask him what planet he comes from when it occurs to you that the better question is "Why are you laughing?" You ask it and then wait patiently while Ronnie gets control. Between snorts of laughter, he answers.

"Well [snort], did you ever hear of a wild goose chase? [snort] I just made up the [snort] bank robbers so I could win the Tall Tale Contest and go to AdventureLand! [snort] Now, I'm sure to win. You two are *such* good sports that I may even invite you to come along with me!"

You've always really *loved* it when someone makes a fool of you, right? No? Well, perhaps there's a way to get even.

Turn to PAGE 64.

"J.J.," you say. "That's a swell tall tale Ronnie made up, but don't you think we can do him one better? How about the *true* story of Ronnie's tall tale PLUS the thrilling, true-to-life finale about how you and I took all of Ronnie's clothes — except for his thermal underwear — and left him to find his own way back to town! We can call it 'Revenge on Danger Mountain'!"

"You can't do that to me! How could I ever face my friends?"

"What friends?"

You and J.J. are going to have no trouble at all deciding how you'll spend your time at AdventureLand.

THE END

Finally, you come out of the tunnel into a huge room, lit by an eerie glow. Is it the crystalline walls and the gigantic stalactites that glow? No, the light appears to come from torches. But the glow, where does that come from?

You walk farther into the room and you realize that the glow is from jewels! A mountain of jewels! There are diamonds and rubies, gold and silver, pearls, opals — you name it, it's there.

"Chief Sitting Elk's treasure! There really is one!" You take a flying leap into the enormous pile of gems. Suddenly the jewels seem to be getting warm, almost hot. Your feet become uncomfortable, burning.

"Hey, wake up!" says J.J. "Your feet are almost in the campfire!"

You sit up with a start. There's no cave, there are no torches, and, alas, no gems. There weren't even any bank robbers! There's only Mr. Marks' monotonous voice, still talking about the camp-out schedule.

". . . then at eight-thirty, campfire; eight-forty-five, community sing; nine-o'clock, moth hunt; nine-thirty, firefly-catching contest; ten-o'clock, taps."

Boy this camp-out is definitely

THE END

So there you are, floating a couple of hundred feet in the air, robbers to the left, police to the right, friends in the line of fire, and you and J.J. are the only ones who can avert certain disaster for your friends, but how??? You try yelling, but the wind carries your voices away.

"How are we going to get their attention?" asks J.J.

"I don't know," you admit. "We're trapped by that crazy lady." Suddenly, you hear a voice from below.

What's that witch lady saying now? Good news or bad? It couldn't be worse than this . . . or could it?

If you fear the worst, whatever that is, turn to PAGE 71.

If you feel things are looking up, turn to PAGE 68.

TOO MUCH!

You and Leslie have both corrected to the right and over goes the canoe. *Splash!*

Well, there you are, treading water, in the middle of Lake Pittiwawa. The police are too far away to hear your shouts and the bank robbers are headed straight toward you!

Now you're *really* sunk!

THE END

Things are looking up, all right! The witch is looking up and it looks like bad news for you! You can hear her now:

"Crazy lady you call me? See how you like this!" You watch the robbers overrun your classmates' campsite while the police run in on the other side and enter the fray. Just as the fighting starts, you feel yourselves moved to high above the lake and suddenly released!

Talk about making a splash!

THE END

Out you go, across the ravine, but you can't reach the other side. The vine brings you back to the ledge.

"Look, let's take hold farther down the vine. That'll give it more length, though it's a tough take-off." So you try again. This time you *almost* reach, but it becomes clear that the vine just isn't long enough and won't be until it grows another 10 feet. However, what you *have* managed to do is to lower yourselves to the same ledge Mr. Marks is on.

"Look, kids!" he says. "I think I see it now! Is it — could it be — a downy-chinned stork? Or maybe the yellow-crested queen-stalking kingfisher?"

Great. How long will it take until that vine grows another 10 feet? Until then, you're stuck with crazy Mr. Marks. Everything's really gone to the birds, hasn't it?

THE END

"Hey, Jackie," you say. "I think the lake is this way. Let's go." You walk a hundred feet or so through the forest and find yourselves on the shore.

"Here's the lake, and, hey, there's a canoe! Can you help paddle the canoe to the other side? I'm sure that's where the police are," says Jackie.

You climb into the canoe, very carefully. Jackie takes the paddle in the stern. You get in the bow. Leslie sits between you. Carefully, quietly, you begin to paddle across Lake Pittiwawa.

In a short time, you are near the middle of the lake. A dark shape suddenly looms before you.

"Look!" hisses Jackie. "There's another boat on the lake. It must be the bank robbers!"

"Where?"

"There, to the left." Jackie points with a paddle and leans as if to make the point more definite. Well, it makes it more definite, for sure! The canoe's going to tip to the left! Watch out!

Stick out your right arm and lean to the right to keep the canoe from going over. Now, turn to PAGE 67 to see if it worked!

There are people who believe that you should always think of the worst possible things that could happen because what *will* happen will be the one thing you didn't anticipate. Think of as many really awful things as you can that could happen to you and J.J., suspended 300 feet in the air.

Now turn to PAGE 39 and see if you've given yourself enough protection.

"Okay, then, let's keep going this way," you say. "Mr. Marks has to be right near here. We should be close to the vans. They're probably right up — uh-oh, the path splits here. Okay, guys, which way now, left or right?"

Suddenly, it seems your options are cut off. There's another BANG! and it's right next to you!!!

Is it the cops or the robbers? Which way will you run?

If you want to run away from the shots, turn to PAGE 83.

If you want to go toward the shots, turn to PAGE 85.

It's harder swimming upstream, against the current, but in this case it seems to you that it's more likely to get you up out of the mountain cave to the outside.

Well it *seems* that way, but it doesn't *work* that way. Suddenly, you realize that you have come right back into the cave where your captors are waiting for you. Clearly, the underground creek will never bring you to safety. Somewhat sheepishly, you three climb out of the river, and find yourselves, once again, facing very few choices. The flickering of the torches catches your eye again. Well, perhaps if you can distract your captors by grabbing a torch and using it as a weapon, you can run out of the cave.

Turn to PAGE 15.

"Yeah, let's go back to the cave and see how long we can string these guys along," says Ronnie.

You all run back in, pretending you've just been frightened out of your wits by the ghost. The anthropologists sympathize with you.

"The reason we jumped you when you first came in," one of them explains, "is that the ghost had just appeared and threatened us. The walls of the cave had begun to ooze with water that formed the pool over there, and the fire you see before you, emerged from nowhere." You are getting a gnawing feeling that this is bigger than a recorder, a projector, and a fan.

Suddenly you hear a voice — very different from the recording you heard before. "You violate the caves of Sitting Elk!" booms the voice. You realize, in case there was any doubt left, that this is Definitely Not Funny. "You are gnats in the eye of Sitting Elk and must be crushed!" With that, the walls of the cave begin to close in on you all. Maybe telling ghost stories in the deep woods late at night wasn't such a swell idea after all. How about a disappearing act? Do you think you can pull one before this cave gets too small for you? If not, this will surely be

THE END

"Ronnie, I've had enough of your practical joking. J.J. and I will go to the creek together. You know where you can go, and you can go there by yourself!"

You're really angry with Ronnie. Well, he deserves it, and you're glad to be rid of him.

Soon, however, you begin to wonder if you're headed the right way. You stop for a moment, confused. But then you hear something to give you confidence. It's the bubbling of water. Or is it? No, it's more like humming. Could it be a person?

"I can't see who or what it *is*," says J.J.

Yeah, well it's probably Ronnie again. If you think so, turn to PAGE 76.

On the other hand, you were pretty rough on him. If you don't think it's Ronnie, turn to PAGE 41.

"I'm sure it's just dumb old Ronnie," you say. "Let's give him the scare of his life!"

You and J.J. devise a plan. You are going to circle around to the right, J.J. to the left. When you get on either side of that humming, you're going to jump him. That'll teach Ronnie a lesson!

It's hard to keep from rustling leaves, but when you move just one foot at a time, pick it up and put it down *very* carefully, you are pretty quiet. Soon, you're both near the humming. Vaguely, you see a large dark figure. It doesn't *really* look like Ronnie, but the shadows of the early morning sun play tricks with your eyes.

You and J.J. both attack, but it's not what you expected — at all! It's not Ronnie. It's not even human. It's just a big old stump, or is it? The first thing you feel is the scratchy bark, but the next thing you feel is the stings of the bees that live in the stump. Yipes! You turn to run, but the bees are really angry now and they continue to attack from the rear.

So much for the idea of sweet revenge on Ronnie. Looks like you and J.J. have gotten it in

THE END

Just when you think you might be able to pull off a great fake faint, you don't have to. You're out like a light and it's for real. Right before you pass out, you notice that all the other people around you are dropping, too.

The next thing you hear is a familiar "Ah-choo," only it's closer than before. You open your eyes to a bunch of weird colored lights in a metallic room. On closer examination, you realize that the "lights" are actually living creatures. They just glow a lot. Sitting beside you are your friends. The bank robbers appear to have been left on Earth. Apparently, you're on the UFO and who *knows* where you're heading!

"Ah-choo!" says one of the glowing creatures.

"God bless you," you respond automatically, but the being looks confused. You can tell that a sneeze means something to the little creatures, but words don't. You open your mouth to try again, but you're so nervous you just stutter, gag, and then cough. At the first hack, the creatures spring into action and immediately bring you all plates of food.

The food is delicious. You didn't know how hungry you were. In fact, you eat so quickly that you start burping.

Turn to PAGE 79.

You try to quiet the burp, but it's just one of those overwhelming belches. Your friends stare at you, horrified, while you apologize, but the light creatures are spurred to a flurry of activity. What have you said this time? *You* may not know, but *they* sure do! They are all burping at each other like crazy and operating the ship's controls. You feel the ship pick up speed . . . heading farther and farther away from Earth! You begin to wring your hands in a nervous manner and absentmindedly start to crack your knuckles.

Screech! The ship stops suddenly and makes a U-turn.

What have you said now? Turn to PAGE 80 to find out.

You look out a porthole from the space-ship and realize that the aliens have brought you back to the forest. A burp sent them away from Earth, but cracking knuckles must mean "Home, James!"

The ship slows and stops. The hatch opens and all of you are lifted out by an anti-gravitational force and set down exactly where you were before. When you are safely on the ground, the hatch shuts and the ship disappears in a flash of light. Gone.

Now, *that's* weird.

"Nobody sneeze," you say.

You look around you and see that in your absence the police actually did arrive in a chopper and have rounded up the robbers and recovered the bank's money.

Now you can get back to the campsite and enjoy the remainder of the camp-out.

Still, you have this nagging feeling of uncertainty. What would have happened if you'd gotten the hiccups?

THE END

Finally, you see the light at the end of the tunnel. Or is it? It's an eerie, flickering light and you realize that it must be a campfire. But whose?

Just as you come to the mouth of the cave, there's a stream of air and *thwap!* an arrow is embedded in the tree trunk right next to your head. *Thwap!* another just misses you on the other side. The three of you run back into the cave to hide.

"Hey! Knock it off!" you call to the pursuers, putting up a good front under the circumstances.

Thwap! Those things even stick into the wall of the cave!

"Boy, did we take a wrong turn!" you tell your friends. You've always had a knack for the obvious. "Let's try to find another way out!"

You go back to wandering through the tunnels in the cave. Luckily, whoever was shooting at you decided not to follow you. You sure hope you can find another way out. Soon.

Turn to PAGE 53 and choose a different path.

You signal Ronnie and J.J. to swim back into the cave and they agree, but you find it's not as simple a matter as you had thought. There is a vast maze of underground creeks and you were incredibly lucky to have followed the branch that took you outside in the first place.

Which way should you go now — upstream or downstream? Which will get you to safety — away from the bank robbers?

Upstream? Turn to PAGE 73.
Downstream? Turn to PAGE 11.

"Eeeeeeeeeeyaheeeeeee!!!" you scream, running as fast as you can away from the bang. Leslie and Jackie follow you without hesitation. For some reason, whoever or whatever made the noise didn't follow you. Maybe it is the bank robbers and they don't want to get involved with kids. Or maybe it's the cops and they don't want any interference. Or maybe the bang was totally unconnected to the robbery. Who knows? Who *cares* as long as you're not being followed — or shot at!

Much to your relief, you're not far from the campsite and soon the glowing fire welcomes you back to your friends.

"Boy, are we glad to see you," says Ronnie Newberger. "I know these woods are full of bank robbers and I think we ought to get out of here. J.J.'s coming with me. Will you join us?"

Have you had enough adventure for one night? Tell Ronnie "No way!" and sit down by the campfire on PAGE 62.

Are you game for more? Go off with Ronnie on PAGE 6.

84

By the time you decide to go into the cave, you don't actually have a choice. The rock has tilted and all three of you tumble down. The entrance is steep and rocky. As you fall, the rocks scrape your knees and elbows.

But the light is getting brighter and brighter and the cave, cool at the entrance, is getting warmer. Finally, it levels off. You and your friends dust yourselves off and walk into a large room.

When you enter, you are amazed at the sight. The room is lit by torches on the walls. A campfire burns at the center of the room and to one side is a stream, apparently an underground branch of the creek above.

Suddenly, three strange men jump out from the shadows and surround you. They are holding bows and arrows aimed at you. You look for a way to protect yourself, but there's nothing — unless you can get to a wall and grab one of the torches, or jump into the water and hope to find the way to the creek above.

If you want to swim for it, jump into the creek on PAGE 28.

If you think you can get a torch, turn to PAGE 15.

"Here. Let's go *toward* the noise. It must be the police," you tell your friends.

That's what *you* think! You walk carefully to the source of the noise and call out, but there's no answer. You find that the noise wasn't any kind of gun at all — just an old wooden door, flapping in the evening breeze, slamming itself against the entrance to a cave. The sign above the entrance says INDIAN TREASURE MINE. Now *that* sounds promising!

You all enter and find yourselves in a labyrinth of deep tunnels. Surely you won't find the bank robbers or the police in here. But what *will* you find?

Enter the cave and learn the secret of the Indian Treasure Mine! Turn to PAGE 53.

"Okay, Mr. Marks. Up until a short while ago, you've always appeared to be a reasonable man. We'll give you the benefit of the doubt. What's this all about?"

"Thanks, kids," he begins. "You see, you only know me as your biology teacher, but when I'm not in the classroom, I'm an undercover agent for the local police. After school, you're liable to find me in an impenetrable disguise, helping to rout the vile criminals who stalk this county and terrorize the good folk of this town. My mission is to protect the peaceful life we Americans treasure!"

Well, that wraps it. Now you *know* he's unglued. Up until this robbery, the main criminal element in town centered around an occasional bicycle theft. Talk about a sleepy town!

Now, your mission is to get Mr. Delusions-of-Grandeur back to the campsite. You should be able to evade the bank robbers until morning, when you really *can* find the vans. Of course, if the robbers do find you first, you'll be protected by Mr. Marks, Super Bird (Brain)! What a comforting thought.

THE END

Scream? How can you scream when you're this scared? You can't even sneeze again, but the UFO does.

"Ah-choo!" Everyone continues to look up, terrified. The robber holding you is so scared, in fact, that he releases you. For what it's worth, you step out of his reach. It turns out to be worth a lot.

"Excuse me," says the voice from the UFO. "I seem to be allergic to something. Anyway, this is the pilot of the police hovercraft. We have you covered completely. Release the youngster, drop your weapons, and surrender! You have no — ah-choo! — choice!"

So it's *not* exactly a helicopter. But then neither — thank goodness! — is it a UFO. Soon the back-up helicopter arrives and the police round up the bank robbers. You and your friends can go back to the campfire — back to the Tall Tale Contest. Somehow, tall tales don't seem as interesting as real ones!

THE END

Didn't anyone ever tell you to be polite to your elders? You shouldn't have gotten this lady angry with you. Remember where you are and how you got there!

"Hey, lady," you say. "I'm really sorry. I didn't mean to insult you."

"Too late," the witch snarls. "Your friends will get *all* the reward money and you two — well, I'm afraid it may be a *long* time before the Rescue Team finds you on the top of that tree." She pauses. "Well, *maybe* that won't be necessary if you can just . . ." *Ah, she's going to relent, you think.*

"It's a pity that tree has so few branches that you can't climb down it," she chuckles. "Perhaps you can just learn to fly, eh?"

Nice going, Big Mouth. You got yourself into this. Looks like you're really up a tree this time.

THE END

"Forget it, Mr. Marks. You've blown your chance to be believed."

"But you don't understand! I was trying to save you!"

"Save us from what, Mr. Marks?" you ask. "Tweety Bird?"

"No, I was trying to save you from the bank robbers! *They* are the ones who knocked me out! They were right there next to me when you found me on the path. I realized that the only way I could get us out of there was by making them believe there was no threat from you *or me*!"

"But the vans! Where are they?"

"Oh, they're right where the robbers found them, but don't worry."

"Don't worry!" you shout. "The robbers probably used them to get away!"

"Oh, no. You see, when they attacked me, I was coming *back* from the vans. I'd gotten to the CB radio and called the police for assistance in getting you all out of the woods. The police said they'd meet us at the vans within minutes. I believe we'll find that who they actually met at the vans was the bank robbers! The coast should be clear for us now. Shall we check on that and then get back to the campsite? We really need to get a good rest. Remember, the bird walk starts at six-thirty!"

Turn to PAGE 90.

"Mr. Marks," you ask. "Do you think we might see the rare Thompson's red-billed night duck?"

"Who knows! I've already seen the elusive light-fingered bank-robbing knapsacker! Anything's possible!"

THE END

You try to sum up the situation.

"Obviously, Mr. Marks was giving us a bunch of phony stuff about the bird and trying to lead us *away* from the vans. The first question is *why* and the next question is what can we do about it."

"Well, if you want to know the why," says Jackie, "you can just lean over the cliff and ask him. He may be a bit nuts, but he's not deaf — and he's listening to us. Aren't you, Mr. Marks?"

"I plead the Fifth Amendment," he calls back.

Gee, that sounds a lot like the kind of answer you might get from a crook.

"Guess we'll have to wait to figure out Mr. Marks' part in all this," you tell Jackie. "Right now we've got to find a way to get off this cliff!"

"I have an idea," says Jackie. "Let's take this thick vine and swing on it, Tarzan-style."

"Great idea! Let's go!" You and Jackie grab the vine, very tightly, test it for strength (it passes) and you are ready to go, but where to?

If you think you can cross the ravine, turn to PAGE 69.

If you think you should be able to swing high enough to reach the top, turn to PAGE 38.

92

This just isn't the kind of book where things go your way. So go ahead and turn to page 27 and stick with the sneezing act. See if you can't fool the bank robbers *this* time. Honestly, *nobody* would have believed that stuff about the plague.

Now practice one more sneeze before you turn to PAGE 27.

Congratulations! You know that three quarters make 75 cents, plus a dime is 85 cents, plus one nickel and three pennies is 93 cents. You're so clever, you could even have a happy ending come up!

Suddenly you see Mr. Marks — and he's not alone. Following him are 10 state police officers.

"Boy, are we glad to see you!" you say. The police round up the bank robbers. Mr. Marks, your friends, and you go back to the campsite. What a story you have for the Tall Tale Contest, but it's not a tall tale!

Later that night, you and your classmates get to talking about where you'll go on your next class outing.

"AdventureLand," you say. "You see, I think I'd like to do something nice, calm, and quiet on the next trip!"

Now, that's really

THE END

Collect All the Twistaplot™ Books and Choose from over 200 Endings!